Disney · PIXAR

TOY STORY

ADVENTURES IN ANDY'S ROOM

Illustrated by the Disney Storybook Artists
Based on the art and character designs created by Pixar

A GOLDEN BOOK • NEW YORK

Copyright © 2010 Disney Enterprises, Inc./Pixar. Original *Toy Story* elements © Disney Enterprises, Inc.
All rights reserved. Slinky® Dog is a registered trademark of Poof-Slinky, Inc. © Poof-Slinky, Inc. Playskool Rockin' Robot
Mr. Mike® is a registered trademark of Hasbro, Inc. Used with permission. © Hasbro, Inc. All rights reserved.
Published in the United States by Golden Books, an imprint of Random House Children's Books, a division of
Random House, Inc., 1745 Broadway, New York, NY 10019, and in Canada by Random House of Canada Limited,
Toronto, in conjunction with Disney Enterprises, Inc. Golden Books, A Golden Book,
and the G colophon are registered trademarks of Random House, Inc.

ISBN: 978-0-7364-2642-8
www.randomhouse.com/kids
Printed in the United States of America
10 9 8 7 6 5 4 3 2

Buzz Lightyear and Sheriff Woody make a great team.

Meet Rex and Hamm!

Andy has many toys.

Woody is Andy's favorite toy.

Woody has a special spot on Andy's bed.

While Andy is away, Woody gathers the toys for a meeting.

Rex is always ready to play!

Bo Peep has her eye on Woody.

Slinky is a loyal friend.

Hamm counts his change.

Andy gets lots of presents at his birthday party.

There's a new toy in Andy's room.

Woody is *not* happy to meet Buzz Lightyear.

Buzz thinks he is a real space ranger—and that he can fly.

Andy loves playing with Buzz.

Rex makes a new friend.

Oh, no—Buzz fell out the window!

Buzz hitches a ride.

"You are just a *toy*!" says Woody.

Buzz and Woody sneak into Pizza Planet.

The toy aliens wonder who will be chosen next.

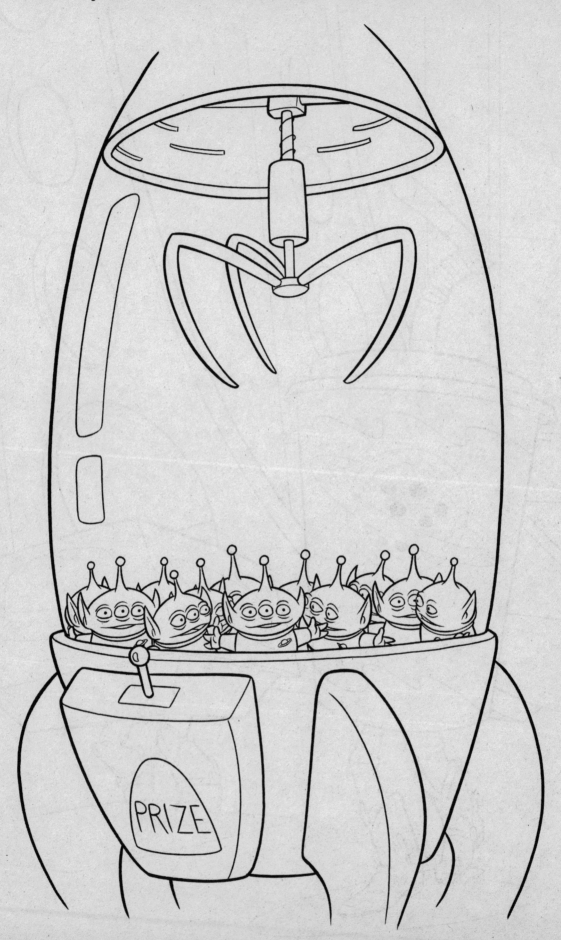

Buzz and Woody become prizes.

Oh, no—it's the toy-torturing Sid!

Buzz and Woody are trapped in Sid's backpack.

Buzz and Woody try to defend themselves.

Sid's mutant toys are scary!

Buzz learns that Woody was right—he is only a toy.

The space ranger attends a tea party.

Sid plans to blow Buzz to pieces!

Woody tells Buzz they must escape and return to Andy.

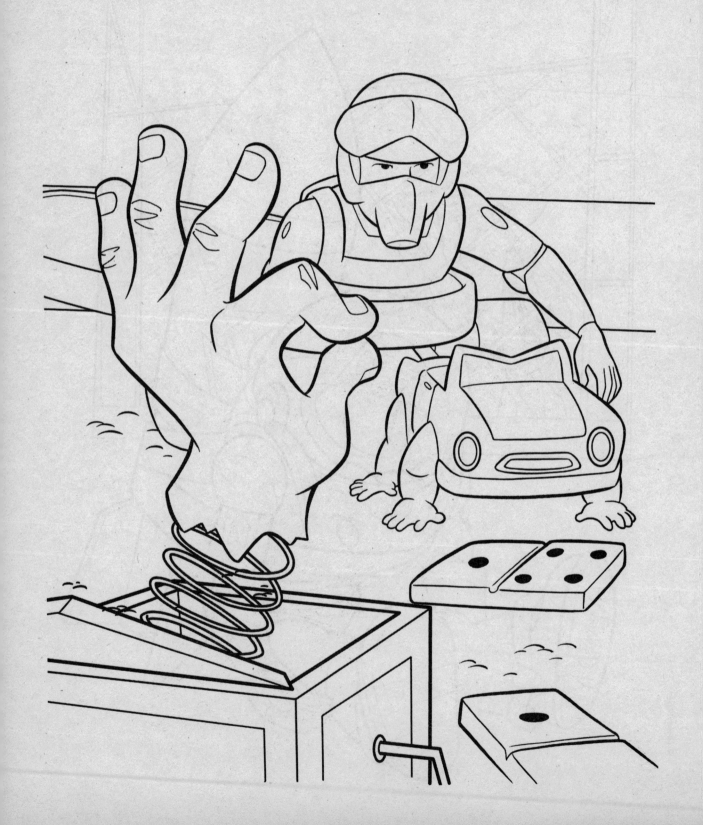

The mutant toys help Woody come up with a rescue plan.

Sid gets ready to blow Buzz up.

"Play nice!" Woody tells Sid.

Sid gets the shock of his life.

Sid has learned his lesson.

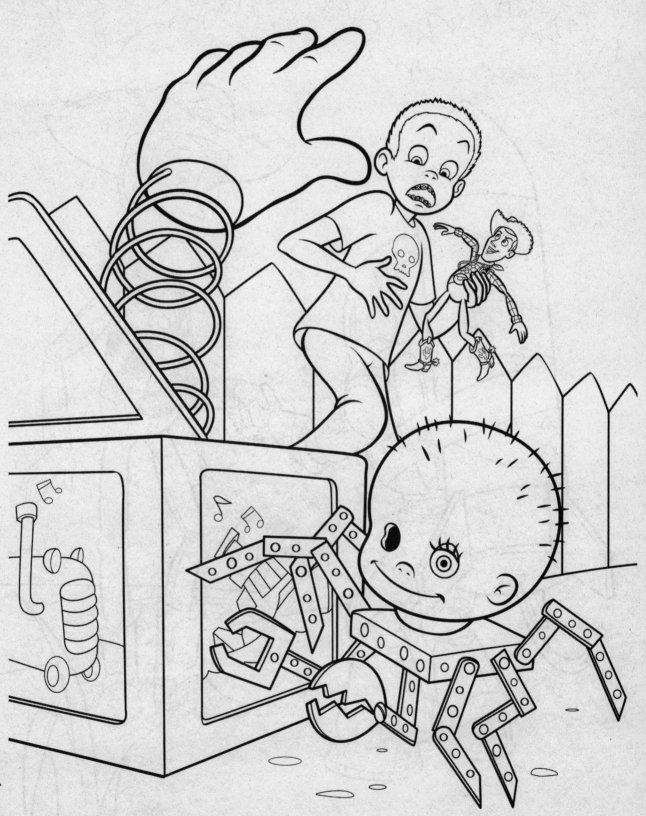

Buzz thanks Woody for a daring rescue.

Andy misses his favorite toys.

Buzz and Woody have to get back to Andy!

The toys run as fast as they can.

"You can do it, Woody!"

The rest of Andy's toys watch out for Buzz and Woody.

RC tries to help Buzz and Woody.

"This isn't flying . . . this is falling with style!"

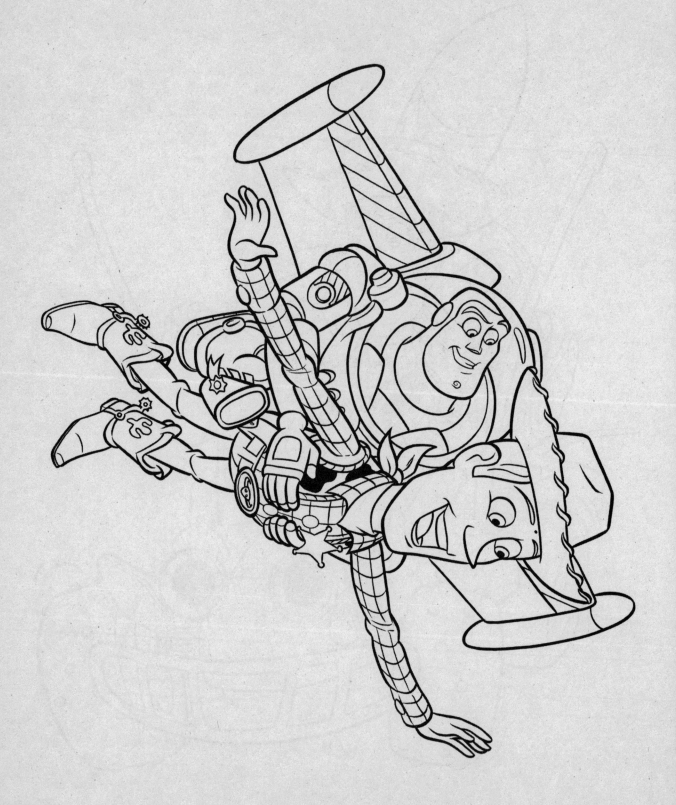

Andy is thrilled to find his favorite toys!

Buzz and Woody are back where they belong.

ZURG

BUZZ

Rex tries to defeat Emperor Zurg.

Andy loves to play with his toys.

Oh, no—Woody's arm ripped!

Woody has been shelved!

Woody finds a broken toy named Wheezy.

Woody is stranded at a yard sale.

Oh, no—Woody has been stolen by Al!

Buzz tries to catch up to Woody's toynapper.

Woody meets Jessie the cowgirl and Bullseye the horse.

The Prospector is glad to see Woody.

Woody discovers that he is a TV star!

Al wakes up to find Woody out of his case.

Soon Woody will look just like new!

Jessie tells Woody that a little girl once loved her.

Jessie was given away many years ago.

Buzz leads Andy's toys on a rescue mission to Al's Toy Barn.

Hamm and Rex explore Al's Toy Barn.

Rex has found the secret to defeating Zurg!

The toys cruise the aisles in search of Woody.

Buzz discovers a Buzz Lightyear display.

Buzz meets a brand-new Buzz.

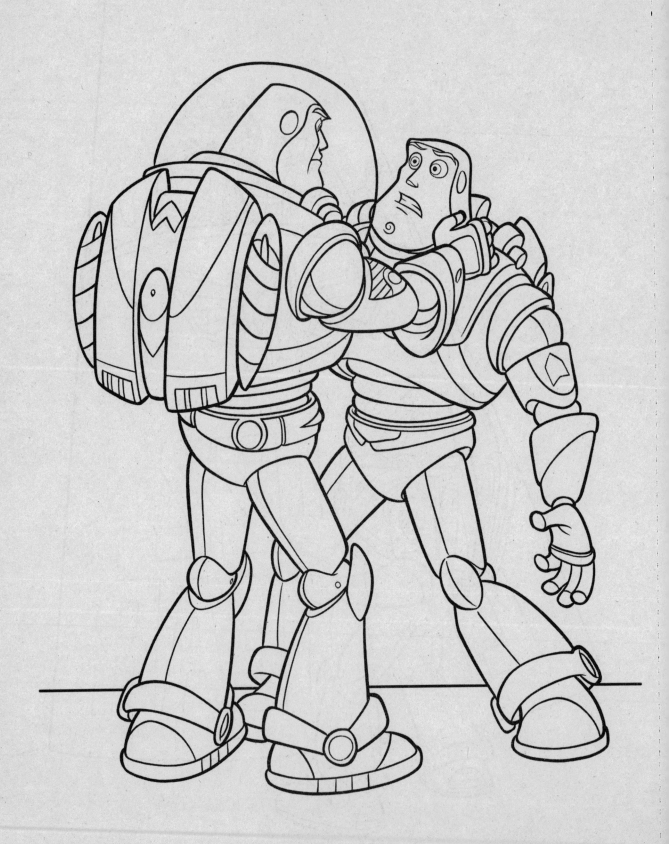

"You're breaking ranks, Ranger!" says New Buzz.

Al plans to send Woody to a toy museum—in Japan!

The toys hitch a ride in Al's bag.

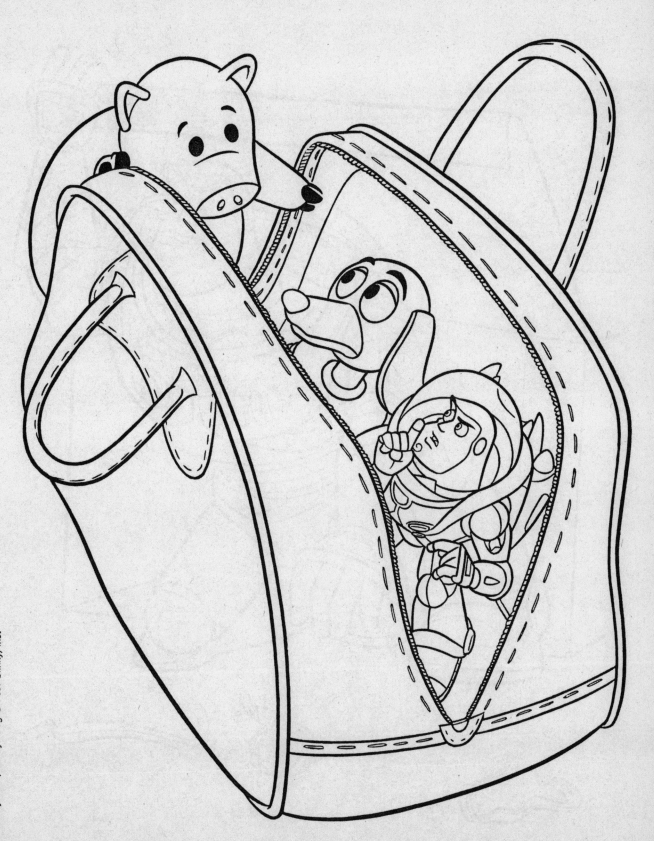

Buzz breaks free.

The toys rush to the rescue!

Woody, Jessie, and Bullseye are the Roundup gang.

Slinky corners the Prospector.

Buzz proves his identity.

Buzz tries to convince Woody to come home.

Woody misses Andy.

The Prospector won't let the Roundup gang leave!

Buzz and Slinky try to pull Woody to safety.

Rex, Slinky, and Hamm borrow a truck.

Buzz has to find Woody!

The Prospector tries to make sure Woody will never escape.

The toys save the day!

"Happy trails, Prospector!"

Oh, no—Jessie is in trouble!

Woody tries to reach Jessie.

Jessie is so glad to see Woody!

The plane is taking off—with Woody and Jessie on board!

Buzz and Bullseye ride to the rescue.

The toys are all safe!

Andy loves his toys—old and new!

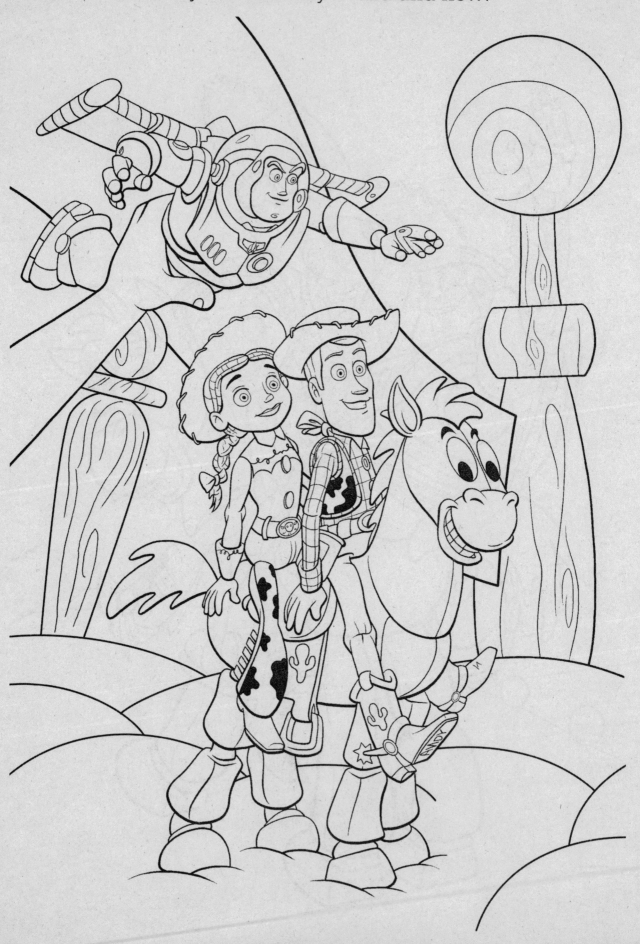